Eukee
The Jumpy Jumpy Elephant

By Clifford L. Corman, M.D. and
Esther Trevino, M.F.C.C.

Illustrated by
Richard A. DiMatteo

Eukee the Jumpy Jumpy Elephant
By Clifford L. Corman, M.D. and Esther Trevino, M.F.C.C.

Illustrations by Richard A. DiMatteo

Eukee's Song © Esther Trevino, M.F.C.C.

ISBN-13: 978-1886941755
ISBN-10: 1886941750

Published by:
Specialty Press, Inc.
300 Northwest 70th Ave., Suite 102
Plantation, Florida 33317
(800) 233-9273
www.addwarehouse.com

Printed by Everbest Printing Co., Ltd.
Guangzhau, China. Postal Code 511458
Date of Production: August, 2009
Cohort: Batch 1

*We dedicate this book to
the parents and children
who are learning the skills
to meet the challenges of
attention deficit disorder.*

Eukee lived in the jungle with his mother and father.

Eukee was very smart, and he liked to play. He chased butterflies, blew bubbles, played hide and seek, and did cartwheels.

Eukee went to school with all his friends.

In school he learned to count, to read, and to write.

Eukee loved school, but he had trouble sitting still. His friends called him the jumpy jumpy elephant. No matter how hard Eukee tried, he just couldn't be still. So his teacher suggested Eukee and his parents go see Dr. Tusk.

Eukee went to see Dr. Tusk with his mother. He reached for a game on the top shelf. The shelves began to shake and games, toys and stuffed animals tumbled down. Building blocks fell on Eukee's head.

"Eukee, you have to be careful," said his mother. "You could hurt yourself."

"I'm sorry mom. I feel jumpy jumpy inside," said Eukee.

Doctor Tusk heard the crash and came out to see if everyone was all right.

"Hi," he said to Eukee. "What's happening out here?"

"I don't know. I just get into trouble a lot," said Eukee.

Doctor Tusk smiled and invited Eukee to come into his office to talk.

Dr. Tusk and Eukee sat down. Dr. Tusk asked Eukee to explain what kind of trouble he gets into.

"I get in trouble because I don't finish The Elephant March at school. After recess, I'm supposed to line up and hold on to the tail of one of my friends. Then we march across the school yard and get a drink of water. Sometimes I forget to hold on, and I push my friends and hit them with my trunk."

"I just feel so jumpy jumpy inside," said Eukee.

"One day, while I was doing The Elephant March, a big yellow butterfly landed on my trunk," explained Eukee. "When it flew away, I followed it into the jungle. I asked it to slow down, but it kept playing hide and seek with me. Hide and seek is so much fun."

"I bet that was more fun than The Elephant March!" said Doctor Tusk.

"And how!" said Eukee. "The Elephant March is so-oo-oo boring. That's why I didn't hear my teacher when she called me. I was having too much fun. I didn't want to stop."

"I see," said the doctor. "Then what happened?"

I ran home to my mother and father. I told them what happened. My dad was upset and said, " 'You need to pay attention in school.' "

"How did you feel?" asked Dr. Tusk.

"I felt bad." I told them, " I'm sorry mom...
I'm sorry dad. I'll do better. Tomorrow
I'll finish the Elephant March."

How did you do the next day?" the doctor asked.

"I started out great. I was keeping in step and holding on to my friend's tail. I was fine, but then Mrs. Ostrich pranced by with her fluffed up feathers, and somehow my trunk got caught in her feathers.

"Then I blew air through my trunk and the feathers danced in the air. My friends joined in and we all got in trouble. Now their mothers won't let them play with me because they say I'm a troublemaker."

"You must have felt terrible," said Dr. Tusk.

"I did. I felt sad, awful. I don't have any friends," cried Eukee.

Eukee put his head down and began to cry. He didn't know what he could do. His parents were getting more and more worried about him. His friends couldn't play with him. He kept getting in trouble at school. All because he couldn't pay attention and felt jumpy inside.

Dr. Tusk went to Eukee and told him not to worry. "Eukee, you are not alone. There are lots of kids who get jumpy inside and have trouble paying attention.

I think I can help you with this problem, but first we have to talk some more and take some tests together."

Dr. Tusk and Eukee talked a lot more that day and his parents brought him to see Dr. Tusk again the next day. They talked and talked and talked. Eukee felt much better after telling Dr. Tusk about his problems. Dr. Tusk asked him so many questions. He got to draw pictures and to put puzzles together. He even did some work on Dr. Tusk's computer. That was the best part.

When they were finished, Dr. Tusk spoke with Eukee and his parents. He turned to Eukee and said, "Eukee, I understand how hard it's been for you." Eukee smiled and his mother looked at him lovingly.

Dr. Tusk explained, "Eukee has trouble paying attention and keeping his mind from wandering and telling his body to stay still. That is why he is so jumpy."

"It's not his fault," said the doctor. "Just like it's not someone's fault if he or she has trouble seeing and needs to wear glasses. It's just the way Eukee's mind works. We call this attention deficit disorder... ADD for short."

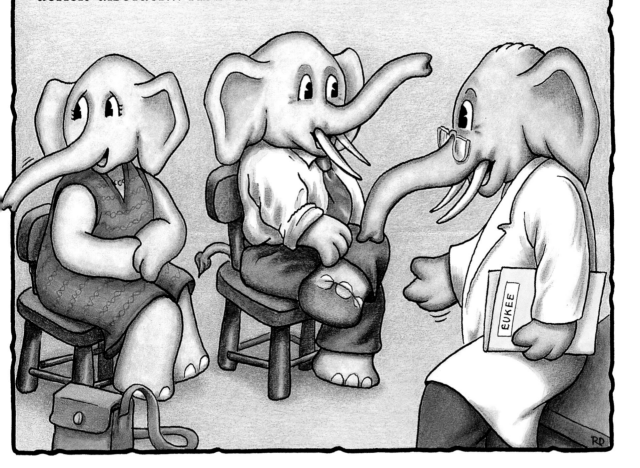

Dr. Tusk said, "Eukee, your parents and your teacher and I will try to help you. We will remind you to slow down when you get too jumpy."

"We will make up a behavior chart to help you at home.

We can give you some medicine. It will help you pay attention better and be less jumpy inside."

Eukee felt much better after he left Dr. Tusk's office. Finally, he understood what made him so jumpy jumpy. He also knew that his parents, his teacher and Dr. Tusk would be able to help him.

Things started working out pretty well for Eukee from then on. He and his parents made up a behavior chart to help him.

Eukee got hugs and smiles from his mother and father. When he did what was on his chart, he got a happy face sticker. When he got enough stickers he could play ball, go for a pizza, or get a prize.

Eukee also did better at school.

His teachers would write on his papers, "Good job... Well done...You're the best!" Soon everyone began to feel better. Nobody called Eukee the jumpy jumpy elephant anymore.

Eukee even learned to finish The Elephant March. He did such a good job, he was chosen to be the leader.

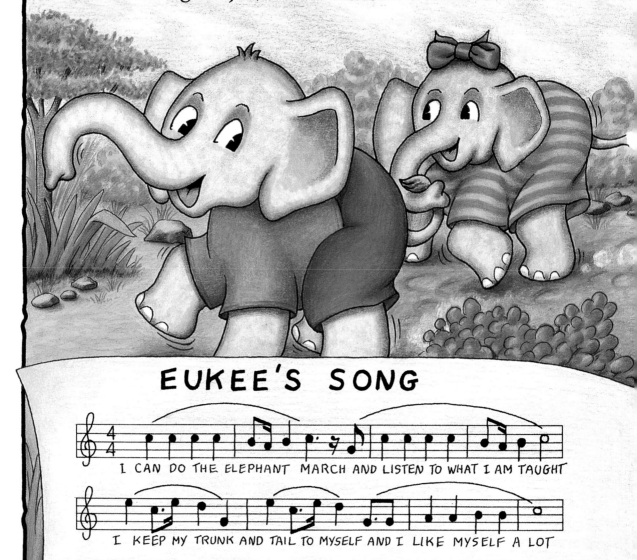

EUKEE'S SONG

I CAN DO THE ELEPHANT MARCH AND LISTEN TO WHAT I AM TAUGHT

I KEEP MY TRUNK AND TAIL TO MYSELF AND I LIKE MYSELF A LOT

And just to make sure he would remember what to do, he made up this song. He sang it to himself every time he did the march.

WATCH ME SEE WHAT I CAN DO WHEN I LISTEN I KNOW WHAT TO DO

NOW I HAVE FUN I HAVE FRIENDS AND I LIKE MYSELF A LOT.

RESOURCES
Other books about attention deficit disorders for children

Gehret, J. (1991) *Eagle Eyes*. New York. Verbal Images Press.

Gordon, M. (1991). *Jumpin' Johnny Get Back To Work.* New York. Gordon Publications, Inc.

Gordon, M. (1991). *My Brother's A World Class Pain*. New York. Gordon Publications, Inc.

Levine, M. (1990). *A Mind of Your Own.* Massachusetts. Educator's Publishing Service.

Moss, D. (1989) *Shelley, the Hyperactive Turtle*. Maryland. Woodbine House, Inc..

Nadeau, K. and Dixon, E. (1991) *Learning To Slow Down and Pay Attention.* Virginia. Chesapeake Psychological Services.

Parker, R. and Parker, H. (1993) *Slam Dunk: A Young Boy's Struggle with Attention Deficit Disorder.* Florida. Specialty Press, Inc.

Quinn, P. O. and Stern, J.M. (1991). *Putting On The Brakes. Young People's Guide To Understanding Attention Deficit Hyperactivity Disorder (ADHD).* New York. Magination Press.

All of the above products are available through the
A.D.D.WareHouse. For more information about these and other
products related to attention deficit disorders, or to receive
a free catalog, call or write:

A.D.D. WareHouse
300 Northwest 70th Avenue
Plantation, Florida 33317
1-800-233-9273 (1-800-ADD-WARE)
305-792-8944